Love is PAIN

MISTY TONEY

authorHOUSE®

AuthorHouse™
1663 Liberty Drive
Bloomington, IN 47403
www.authorhouse.com
Phone: 1 (800) 839-8640

Published by AuthorHouse 10/07/2016

ISBN: 978-1-5246-4438-3 (sc)
ISBN: 978-1-5246-4436-9 (hc)
ISBN: 978-1-5246-4437-6 (e)

Library of Congress Control Number: 2016916787

Print information available on the last page.

Credit for the quote / website used https//www.goodreads.com/tag/evil
Facts about domestic violence found on: thehotline.org/resources/statistics
And wisqars.cdc.gov
For more information about Misty D. Satterfield, please visit: Satterfield_Editions.com

TABLE OF CONTENTS

I would like to take this page to talk about the publication of Love is Pain. The subject of domestic violence isn't a laughing matter this is a subject that for personal reasons is close to my heart. There is never a reason for anyone to lay hands on another person out of anger. If you know anyone dealing with domestic violence, please help them get help.

National Domestic Violence Hotline: 1-800-799-7233

(TTY) 1-800-787-3224

I am dedicating this page for just this reason. At the bottom of this page you will find the National Domestic Violence help hotline. to call and get help. And if you don't want to get help this way. Please talk to someone. Don't become a statistic please.

Statistics found on: https//www.wiqars.cdc.gov

And: thehotline.org/resources/statistics

On average twenty-four people per minute are victims of rape, physical violence, or stalking by an intimate partner in the United States. That is more than twelve million women and men over the course of a year.

Nearly half of all women and men in the U.S. have experienced psychological aggression by an intimate partner in their lifetime. Forty-eight point four percent and Forty-eight point eight respectively.

Author of Love Is Pain Misty D. Satterfield

DEDICATION

I WOULD LIKE to take the time to thank you for purchasing my first book. This subject matter is dear to my heart. I hope you enjoy reading this as much as I enjoyed writing it.

In addition, if you enjoyed reading Love is pain please look for Taken by Evil the follow up book to Love is Pain. Once again Thank you for your support!

I would like to thank my family and friends for being supportive. And a special thanks goes out to Betsy, Shawn, Dakota, Melissa, and Mark. thanks for believing in me and pushing me when I needed it I love you all.

And to for creating the book cover. Thank you for doing such a great job!

And to anyone out there if you have a dream know that anything is possible. All you have to do is put in the work. And if anyone tells you that it can't be done. Prove them wrong!

Thank everyone again so much support.

Quote

"Any intelligent fool can make things bigger, more complex and more violent. It takes a touch of genius—and a lot of courage— to move in the opposite direction."

By Albert Einstein

PREFACE

I REMEMBER WHEN I was a little girl my mom telling me that one day I would grow up and find my Prince Charming. She used to read me fairy tales. There was always a damsel in distress and some perfect guy that comes along and saves her because in the end they were meant for each other. We all know the kind of books I am talking about. The ones that as we grow older we realize that never in a million years could any of those things have possibly taken place.

But as a young woman you still look for the grand gestures and the possibility that the person you are meant to be with is out there. What happens when you think you found that person only for them to turn into a monster. That is capable of unspeakable things. This actually happens more than most people think. It happened to me and I almost didn't survive it. My Fairy tale had turned into a nightmare. One that doesn't seem to end.

So I am going to start at the beginning so that you understand I was just like everyone else. I fell in love and thought I was going to have a great life and someone to share that with. But sometimes things aren't what they seem I met him in college his name was Jason but I called him Jay. And yes he was handsome but he was also arrogant and I didn't like him at first. But we ended up being partners in chemistry class. I actually thought that it was a sign how corny is that. So after studying together for a few months I realized he wasn't who I thought he was. He was kind, sweet, and funny. We even liked a lot of the same things.

One day after class I had mustard up enough courage to ask him on a date. I wasn't sure if he would say yes. But he did and after that we were inseparable until graduation. That's when he told me he was going to join the military. A lot of his friends were doing it and he said that it would help his chances of getting a better job when he got out. He said most people have a hard time landing a job right out of college.

And he was right it took me six months and I took business which is really practical compared to some of the other majors my friends had taken. Then he told me he would be leaving in six months. I didn't want him to go but I wasn't going to hold him back either. I had seen other girls do that kind of thing and it never ended well. I can't even begin to explain how much I loved him. But like the old saying goes if you love them let them go and if they come back to you it was meant to be.

We went out the night before he left for boot camp. We ate Italian food which is my favorite and when we were done there we went to see a movie. We got back to my apartment and sat down on the couch to watch television. We weren't there long before we got swept away with one another and ended up finding ourselves in the bedroom. And with me knowing that he would soon be gone for six months made everything even more intense.

When we were done in the bedroom we got in the shower together where he washed my hair and lathered me up with soap. I had to pull away or we probably wouldn't have made it out of the shower. When we finally did make it out of the shower. I began drying my hair. He went to the bedroom to get his clothes or so I thought. But when I was done

I saw him standing in the doorway of the bathroom wearing nothing but a towel.

He looked at me smiled and got down on one knee. Elizabeth Pritchard will you be my wife he asked. I began to cry and I thought at that moment my mom was right. I had found my happily ever after. Little did I know it would soon turn into my own nightmare.

CHAPTER ONE

Saved

I AWOKE NOT knowing where I was. I couldn't swallow anything. Every time I tried began gagging. My eyes darted around the room wildly. Then they landed on a man standing in front of me in a white coat. Easy, it will be over in a minute he said. I am almost done. I was frightened but I stayed unnaturally still. Afraid to even breathe until he said that he was done. Even when the discomfort had eased. I still didn't move until he said he was finished. Finally I was able to swallow without gagging but it was still extremely painful. It felt like I had been swallowing shards of glass.

As I looked around the room I saw nurses, doctors, and medical equipment everywhere. That's when I realized I was in a hospital. I tried to move but my body was wracked with pain. Causing me to scream. What happened to me? Was I in a car wreck? Oh my god I can't remember what happened to me I thought to myself. The room was spinning, my head was pounding, and suddenly I felt like I couldn't breathe.

One of the machines started to beep. That's when one of the doctors called a nurse that was in the room over to where he was standing. Then he began giving her orders. But my hearing was muffled and I couldn't make out anything he was saying. She almost ran out of the room. The nurse returned a few moments later with two syringes in hand. That's when I noticed the tubing running from my neck to a IV pole. I'm giving you something for the pain and to help you rest she said. A few minutes later my eyes started to get heavy as I slowly drifted asleep.

Sometime later I came too. Only to find that one doctor still remained in the room. He looked at me and then walked away without saying a word. I needed to speak to him but I wasn't sure that I could endure the pain no matter how much I needed answers. That's when I saw him walking over to the bed that I was lying in. Then he began lifting the head of my bed. He didn't speak. But I noticed he was holding a cup of ice water with a straw that had been sitting on the bed side table. Once he finished adjusting the bed he held the straw up to my lips. Drink, it will help he said.

I knew that I was drinking it fast but I couldn't stop myself. My mouth was so dry and it was also helping with the pain I was feeling in my throat. He smiled and pulled the straw away slowly. That should help but you don't want to drink too much too fast he said with a smile. Then he walked over to the bedside table and sat the cup back down and asked is that better? Still afraid to speak I nodded yes. I knew I had to try to speak again. But I still wasn't sure if I could handle the pain.

Thankfully before I could speak he began introducing himself. My name is Dr. Michaelson. I have been you're doctor ever since you were brought into the emergency room. I was assigned to your case he said smiling. I imagine it hurts to speak right now. That is because of the breathing tube I removed this morning. It was put in after you arrived to the emergency department. You were in critical condition when you arrived and no one was sure that you would make it. You're a very lucky young lady he said.

We discovered that your skull had been fractured and there was some swelling of the brain. You also had two fractured vertebrae in your neck and three in your spine. You had a punctured lung on the right side, some internal bleeding, and your right hand and wrist were both broken. You had so many breaks and fractures. I had never seen a person with injuries so severe. Both ankles, your right leg, three broken ribs, and last but not least severe lacerations covered your entire body. In my twenty years here I haven't seen anything like it he said.

I just laid there listening in disbelief. As he continued to speak. We were concerned about your blood pressure becoming too high. Because of the pain and the surgeries that we had to do to repair everything. Also we were worried that you would move and possibly injure yourself even further. That is why I made the decision to put you in a medically induced coma. That's when we put the breathing tube in.

Once you were breathing on your own again and we were sure that there would be no more damage we were able to ease up on the sedatives. But don't worry we will do are best to keep the pain under control he said.

He paused for a moment waiting for me to speak. All I said was how long... How long what he asked? How long have I been like this? He said two weeks....

CHAPTER TWO

Identity Crisis

Do you have any more questions he asked? Who am I and what happened to me I asked? Concern filled his eyes as he said I can tell you what I know but I am sure Detective Jones will fill you in tomorrow. He knows more than I do. When you were brought in you had an ID and three dollars in your back pocket. The identification and money was put in evidence with the rest of your things. But the ID helped us to identify you.

A man named Joel Martin discovered you on the side of old highway eighty-two. Detectives told me that the man was taking his children to school and noticed an object covered in blood on the side of the road. Thinking it was a deer he just kept going. But on his way back he stopped to make sure.

After getting out of the truck and walking closer he realized it wasn't a deer as he first thought. He checked you're pulse. Once he realized you were alive he called it in and stayed with you until the medics and officers arrived. I felt tears filling my eyes. I tried to blink them back but they started fall and before I knew it I began to cry uncontrollably. The doctor said you need some rest this has all got to be overwhelming for you. He hit the call bell on the side of my bed and told the nurse to bring my night time medications.

I looked up and saw the nurse entering the room with more medications to put in my IV. She said this will help you rest. I started to protest but I soon felt myself starting to slip away. But before I lost consciousness I heard the nurse say Elizabeth...

The next morning, I awoke to Dr. Michaelson knocking on the door to my room. He didn't wait for me to answer before walking in. Good morning Elizabeth, he said walking over to the bed I was confined too. I was right I did hear the nurse say my name last night I thought to myself. Then I thought it couldn't have been Melissa, Mandy, or Heather no it had to be Elizabeth. When I remember who my mother is I need to thank her for that one I thought and gave the doctor a polite smile.

How are you today he asked? I feel like I have been beaten to death. I guess he didn't care for my description because he gave me a strange look. And then said well I guess you were. Is that what they think happened to me I asked? That is what happened to you he said. I wasn't hit by a car I asked? I mean I was found on the side of the road right? The injuries you have couldn't have been sustained by a car he said pointedly. You're sure I asked him feeling confused? Yes, Elizabeth one hundred percent sure he said as his eye brows came together.

Do you know my last name I asked? Pritchard he replied. Do they know who did this to me I asked? No not yet but Detective Jones will be by today he said and he should be able to fill you in on the investigation.

Thank you I replied. Sure thing he said as he turned to walk out the door. Suddenly he stopped at the door and said by the way Elizabeth it will come back. What will come back I asked? Your memory he said before disappearing into the hallway.

Chapter Three

Making a Friend

Between sleeping and answering questions for the doctors and nurses there isn't a whole lot I can do. So now every day I wake up and write in this journal Dr. Michaelson gave me. I know that he is hoping that it will help with my memory. He gave it to me two days after I awoke from the coma. I have been here now for a total of three weeks. That is counting the two weeks that I was in the coma and I am now coming up on my fourth week. In that time, I have learned a lot. Yet I still remember nothing before waking up here.

I have learned my name is Elizabeth Pritchard. I was found on the side of an old country road beaten to the point of death. I am in a hospital in North Carolina which is where I am from according to my driver's license. I still have no idea who did this to me. Or even where I live? The address on my driver's license was a dead end.

Well not a total dead end I guess the manager of the apartment complex said that I moved out over four years ago. Right after I graduated from college. But that he had not seen me since then and there was no forwarding address. At least that's what the detectives keep telling me when they stop by every day in hopes I will remember at all.

They say that is all they have come up with for now. I think they are waiting for me to fill in the blanks for them. At this point I have no idea how long I will be here. I'm healing but slowly and even if I was healed completely. I would not rush things. For one I have no idea where home is and two I have only three dollars an I.D., and a pair of blood soaked clothes.

I keep having little flashes of people, places, and things. I think they may be memories but I have no way to be sure what they are. They continue to tell me I will get my memory back but I am not so sure. Meanwhile there is not much I can do so I pass my time writing in this journal and making small talk with the nurses and doctors here.

I have also made a friend or the closest thing to a friend you can have in this situation. Considering I have no idea who I really am. His name is Christian. He is one of the paramedics that brought me here. He comes to check on me every night before he goes home. It gets lonely here and when he is here I don't feel like I am so alone. One of the nurses even told me that he came to see how I was every night even when I was in a coma.

And that's how it started but now we talk about other things besides my health. We talk about my day which is nowhere near as entertaining as his is obviously. I have come to look forward to hearing about his day. It gives me something to think about besides how I am stuck here in a hospital bed. He has also been asking me questions hoping to help with my memory or lack of memory I should say.

At times it can be very frustrating. And I am not the best at hiding my frustration. But I try my best not to take it out on him. He is the closest thing to a friend I have and I may not remember anything but I am smart enough to know I can't afford to lose the only friend I have.

Besides it's actually amusing when he comes to visit me. All of the nurses either start jumbling up their words or blushing when he is around. And with the lack of entertainment around here it is kind of fun to watch. If I wasn't so busy trying to piece my life back together. I would probably be acting like a teenage girl with the rest of them.

I can't really blame them he is kind of hot. You know the type. The whole time you are dating you are trying to figure out what is wrong with them. The ones you see that are still single and you think he is either gay or has raging mommy issues. He has black hair, dark blue eyes, and of course he is in perfect shape.

Okay I admit it he is wicked gorgeous. So gorgeous that sometimes I find myself thinking of what it would be like to be someone he could be attracted too. But I'm not fooling myself into believing that could ever be a possibility. I know what I look like right now. And there is not a place on my entire body including my face that isn't either swollen, bruised, or both. Besides I have enough to worry about without ever going there.

Like I have so much going for me. I'm a homeless twenty-seven-year-old amnesia patient that knows absolutely nothing about myself. Oh wait that's right I know my name. Yeah I'm a real catch alright! I'm just glad to have him as a friend.

CHAPTER FOUR

Dreams or memories

I FINISHED WRITING and put my journal away when I saw Mrs. Nurse I am better than everyone else walking towards my room through the doorway. And no I haven't taken the time to learn their names. I however have learned most of their attitudes and personalities. No one can really blame me though. I just learned my own name a week ago.

I am sure she is on her way in to give me more medication that will knock me out. Like two weeks in a coma wasn't enough sleep. I guess I should be used to it by now but I feel like a child that doesn't want to take a nap. But I have learned something else during my stay here and that is that arguing doesn't get me anywhere with these people.

So when she came in to give me the medication I didn't say a word. She smiled and said I am here to give you some medication my dear. Once she was done she turned and disappeared into the hallway. A few moments later my body relaxed my eyes were getting so heavy I could not keep them opened any longer. I felt myself slipping into the darkness.

Every night I dreamed of his face. I did not know who he was or why he was so angry with me. But he was always screaming at me. He was so close I felt his hot breath on my face. I was just standing there frozen with fear. I didn't know why this man frightened me but I had never felt so afraid of anyone or anything. Who are you I tried to ask? But I couldn't get the words to come out. Who was this man? Why do I continue to dream about him? And why does this man scare me so much?

I suddenly awoke from the dream but I was unable to move it was as if I was paralyzed. I tried to speak but nothing would come out except this time I was awake. What is happening I thought. Once the fear released me from its grip. I realized I was screaming but I didn't know how long I had been screaming for or even when I began screaming. It was like a delayed reaction.

The night shift nurse ran in I was crying and shaking all over. This had been a reoccurring theme the past few nights. Dr. Michaelson says he thinks they are repressed memories that are trying to break through. He also believes that since the memory is terrifying me that my mind is trying to keep them from resurfacing. And that all the stress was causing something similar to sleep paralysis.

After a week of the nightmares continuing Dr. Michaelson had a psychologist start coming to see me every morning. He said that way the memories or nightmares would still be fresh in my mind. Of course he asked if I would mind speaking with someone first. As if I really had a choice in the matter. It was getting worse though I never slept through the whole night anymore not even when they gave me medication to sleep. I woke up screaming bloody murder every night. At this point even I knew I needed a shrink. I thought I was going crazy. I could tell by the way the night shift nurses looked at me that they were ready to get me my own personalized straight jacket.

Meanwhile I'm still confined to this bed. The only thing I have to look forward to are Christian's visits. He avoids asking me about my dreams though. I am not sure if someone told him not to ask me about them but whatever the reason is I am thankful he doesn't. And I avoid asking him why he still comes to see me every day because I am scared of hearing what I already know. That he feels sorry for me. I may have amnesia but I am not stupid enough to let that go no matter the reason behind his friendship.

CHAPTER FIVE

Alone

I WAS STARTLED when I heard a knock at the door. I looked up as Dr. Michaelson was made his way into my room. How are you today Elizabeth he asked as he walked over to where I was lying in bed? I said as good as can be expected. How is your pain he said searching my face for the slightest sign of me not telling the truth? Better than it was I said. But that's what I always said when I was asked. Mostly because I was tired of all the medications they were giving me.

He smiled and laughed a little so should I write on here patient thinks she is superwomen he said motioning to his clipboard. I said no but you can write patient thinks she's storm from X men then I laughed a little. And pain exploded through my body and I could not help the small scream that escaped. He said don't worry you will be ready for physical therapy in no time. I have been here going on four almost five weeks now but I knew six weeks was when he was planning to start the physical therapy.

I wanted to tell him where he could put his physical therapy. But there was no reason to take any of this out on poor Dr. Michaelson. He had his own problems. He stood about five foot seven, almost bald and he always acts like he is all jacked up on too much caffeine. It is so obvious he has a thing for nurse I am better than everyone else. Who's name by the way is Rhonda. I know I said I wasn't going to learn names. Seeing that I haven't known my own all that long. But hey it's the only entertainment I have here. Maybe I am losing it. Who knows I may have been crazy all along. Until my memory returns I guess we will never know.

After Dr. Michaelson was gone Rhonda had returned to the room with four syringes in hand but before she could say anything I said let me guess. Time for my afternoon nap I said jokingly. She smiled and said who told you. I just smiled back. She began to put the medicine in my IV line. Before I knew what was happening I was slipping into my nightmare once again

This dream was different though. I watched myself looking in a mirror. I was feeling under my eyes and rub my fingertips over each bruise. My eyes were swelling closed. I said to myself I have to get out of here or he is going to kill me. I went to a closet and grabbed a bag and grabbed anything I could carry. Once I filled the bag I hid it in the closet underneath somethings. I heard someone trying to get in the door I wet my hair and pulled a towel around me and walked out of the bathroom.

Didn't you hear me knocking I heard him saying. No I didn't I replied. What were you doing he asked? Nothing I was just taking a shower I said. Really? Yes, I replied. He walked toward the closet door and looked at me to see if I showed any type of reaction at all. I was trying to remain passive. Suddenly he stopped and turned back around and walked up to me slowly. He stopped in front of me and smiled and then grabbed the back of my hair wrapping it around his hand. It felt like he was going to rip the hair right out of my head. That's when I smelled it. He had been drinking again my stomach began to twist into knots.

I screamed for him to let go but he just tightened his grip more. Why are you lying he asked? I was sobbing uncontrollably and my voice was shaky when I yelled I am not lying please stop your hurting me. Hurting you he said in an infuriated tone. He continued on saying everything is about you isn't it. What about me he asked? What about you I said. Don't you think you're hurting me he said as he let go of my hair and pushed me into the wall.

How could I possibly hurt you I asked? That's when I saw the look and prepared myself for what was coming. As I balled up against the wall he screamed look at me! When I didn't look up he struck the wall leaving an opening where his fist had crashed through. He screamed once again for me to look at him! Now he was standing over me with his fist drawled back prepared to strike. I begged no please don't. But he had no mercy as he continued to strike me with one blow after another.

Once again I woke up screaming tears running down my face. I looked at the clock and realized it was way past time for Christian to come. He has never missed even one night. I laid there realizing for the first time since waking here that I was really truly all alone.

CHAPTER SIX

Confusion

I KNEW THAT it was a little past seven p.m. because they just brought my dinner trey up. I didn't look up when the lady came in because I didn't want anyone to see me this way. Besides I couldn't eat right now. I would probably just get sick I never really had a stomach of steel. So I pushed the trey to the other side of the table that it had been placed on so that I wouldn't have to look at it anymore.

I had slept longer than I usually would even though the nightmare was way more intense than the others and now I felt excruciating pain coursing through my whole body. I must have slept through medication time because it was starting to wear off. I didn't like to bother the nurses. And I didn't know who my nurse even was since I had slept through shift change.

I felt like I was getting ready to blow chunks and I knew then it would be worse for the both of us if I didn't just hit the call bell. Once I saw Jenifer enter the room I breathed a sigh of relief. Don't get me wrong I have had a lot of good nurses but I can tell that most of them lose their patients with me easily. Between me waking up screaming like a banshee all through the night. And the medications they have to come in to give me every few hours. Well let's just say I can't blame them.

But it's not like I have any control over any of this. So it just makes me feel worse when I see them getting annoyed with me. Hell I am frustrated enough for all of us. But that's exactly why Jenifer is my favorite night shift nurse. She never gets irritated with me and she always checks on me often enough that I never have to call and bother her. It's not that I think they really minded if I called them I just knew they stayed very busy. And I don't want to interrupt whatever they may be doing for someone else.

Jenifer had a huge smile on her face which was normal at the beginning of her shift. I have some fresh water and something for the pain and nausea she said as she entered the room. Jenifer has anyone nominated you for sainthood lately I asked? She smiled and said I wouldn't go that far. I came by with your medicines earlier but you were sleeping and Dr. Michaelson said you haven't been getting very much sleep. So I didn't want to wake you she said. Next time I will though because when the medicine wears off like this it's harder to keep the pain under control. I just smiled and shook my head in agreement.

How is your pain she asked? Not thinking I was completely honest and said I feel like I have beaten to death. Jenifer looked away like she was uncomfortable. I really needed to stop saying that I was thinking to myself. Her smile started to disappear. I smiled and said I am sorry definitely a bad choice of words. I keep forgetting that's what landed me here I said. She gave me a look of understanding as she finished pushing the medicines into my IV and said I will be back in about an hour. I replied okay as she was walking towards the door. She looked back once more before disappearing into the hallway.

It was now eight thirty p.m. I just sat there in bed watching the clock before I knew it was nine p.m. I was beginning to worry. Christian has never missed a visit without telling me he was going to ahead of time. This just wasn't like him. As I sat there watching the clock my mind was going from one crazy scenario to another. I could just kick myself! What are you doing I thought? He isn't obligated to come see you. He saved your life isn't that enough! Really what did I expect he isn't my boyfriend he is just a friend I told myself!

A friend that doesn't owe you anything I thought. That's when the hot tears started streaming down my face. I was so confused did I have feelings for Christian other than friendship? No I am just hurt and worried. I couldn't do this to myself. I was exhausted I reached over to shut off the light. Before I knew it the darkness took hold once again. And so did the nightmare.

CHAPTER SEVEN

Found

I found myself standing in a bathroom staring at myself in the mirror. Both of my eyes were almost swollen shut. My lips were swollen and bloody. I pushed my hair back and grazed my right ear with my hand. My hand felt wet so I brought my hand back down to see what was causing my hand to feel so wet. There was blood covering my hand. I started crying so hard that I couldn't breathe. Suddenly I heard someone jiggling the door knob. Then nothing there was just this eerie silence. I jumped at the sound of someone pounding on the door. The sound was so loud that I thought the door was going to fall down.

I was trying to control my breathing and silence my sobbing. I didn't want whoever was doing this to hear me. So I hobbled to the wall farthest away from the door and with my back facing the wall I quietly slid down to the floor. I heard someone calling out my name but it was muffled and I couldn't make out who it was. My ears started ringing. The pounding on the door stopped. My vision was blurry, my eyes continued to swell shut, and my hearing was completely gone in my right ear now. The pounding on the door startled me again. I sat there watching as the door knob shook.

The crying intensified I had no control I was crying so hard my whole body shook. I was trying to breathe but it was becoming harder to fill my lungs with air by the minute. I knew the door wouldn't hold much longer. So I got up and got into the tub. I don't know why but I felt safer as if I was hidden. I heard more last hit to the door and I could see it swing open from behind the shower curtain and then I saw his face the same angry face and green eyes I have been seeing for weeks now every time I went to sleep.

I awoke screaming again my face was soaked from where I had been crying in my sleep. Jenifer came running into the room with syringes in hand. She began giving me the medication before she even spoke. I was still hysterical she pushed my hair out of my face and handed me a wash cloth for my face. She was rubbing my back and saying there, there, it's not real.

But I knew it was very real. What bothered me more than anything else was he knew my name. That's when I heard a voice that sent the worst kind of chill running down my spine. It was the voice from my dreams oh my god maybe I am going crazy. I was sitting up in bed when I heard the same voice saying don't worry I'm here with you everything is going to be okay now. My eyes quickly scanned the room. I looked to the man in the chair by the window it was dark but there was enough moonlight streaming through the window for me to know it was...it was him......

CHAPTER EIGHT

Fear

I sat there frozen with fear. I just sat there with my mouth gapping open staring at the face that had haunted dreams for weeks. Lizzy it's me I'm here now and I promise I'm not leaving your side he said. I don't know where it came from but I heard someone screaming. Oh shit it's me I'm the one screaming. When I realized I was screaming I stopped and only one word came out. No! He sat there staring at me but I looked away. I wasn't sure who he was I just know that I never wanted to see his face again. Jenifer broke the awkward silence. Elizabeth really needs her rest maybe you could come back tomorrow she said to him.

He replied of course if that's what Lizzy wants. He turned to me with a questioning look on his face. This man frightened me and I have no idea where the courage came from but I looked him in the eye squared my shoulders. Then I asked who are you? Why would I want you to stay? My voice was a little shaky but he didn't know it was because I was afraid of him or at least that's what I hoped. He had a surprised even a shocked look on his face. I am your fiancé.

I felt as if all of the air had been sucked out of the room. I was completely overwhelmed with different emotions. I mean how am

I supposed to respond to that? That's when something happened! I remembered who he was or at least his name. Any other time I would be excited that I remembered anything. But right now I wished I could forget him completely. I really need to calm down. Why is he here now? I needed answers I thought. I looked over to where he was now standing and said Jay?

He smiled and said thank god they said that you might not remember me. He took a step closer as he did I jumped further away from pulling the sheet close to my chest remembering how frightened I was of him in my dreams. He looked like he had just realized that even though I remembered his name I did not remember him. Or maybe he just realized I was scared of him. Whatever the reason he stopped I was thankful that he didn't come any closer. When he stopped moving he spoke again his voice had softened as if not to startle or frighten me any more than he already had. I knew that when you saw me you would remember he said. The doctor told me that sometimes seeing someone familiar can be the key to getting your memory back. Jay I said I don't remember you...

CHAPTER NINE

Deception

H E WAS PACING back and forth slowly running his fingers through his hair. I am sorry it took me so long to find you he said. I mean what kind of fiancé goes out of town on business and comes back to find his future wife gone and just assumes that she left him. I thought you were upset about me going out of town and went to stay at your moms for a while. And I just wanted to give you some space. But when your mother called and said that she called your cell phone and a Detective Jones answered and began asking her a lot of questions but he refused to tell her why he had your phone.

I immediately went to talk to him myself. He continued on as I sat there listening trying to fit the pieces together. I was deep in thought when I heard him say Lizzy. I looked up and said I'm listening. They wouldn't tell me anything he said. They did however interrogate me for hours like I was a suspect. Still I cooperated thinking that they would let me see you or at least tell me where and how you were.

Lizzy I promise I tried to find you as soon as I knew you were really missing. I'm so sorry he said. I had to get my lawyer to threaten the detectives and the hospital. They wouldn't even tell your mother where you were or if you were even alive. She was absolutely beside herself. She boarded a plane an hour ago. Right after I called her to let her know you were okay. I am supposed to pick her up when she arrives. But I can have someone else do it if you want me to stay. I swear from now on I'm not leaving unless you tell me too he said.

Jenifer cleared her throat. I had forgotten she was still in the room. But I was glad that she didn't leave me alone with him. She chimed in saying looks like you have a good one here Elizabeth. A good what? I thought to myself. Then she smiled at Jay and said she really does need her rest. As you could imagine this is all is very overwhelming for her.

I had to stop myself from laughing. Overwhelming I thought to myself. That's what this is because frankly I feel like I am about to have a breakdown of massive proportions. Although I am sure the shrink will be loving all of the progress I have made. In fact, he's probably downstairs decorating the room next door to his office for me right now. Crazy thing is right now I would be okay with that.

Pulling me back into the conversation I heard Jay asking me if that was what I wanted again? All I could manage was a quick nod yes. He stood there a moment looking at me. Finally, he said okay I will go then and let you get some rest dear. Something about the way he said dear and Lizzy made my skin crawl. This time I managed to reply okay. He started to come closer but after seeing me squirm further back he must have thought better of it and said goodnight. Then he turned and just like that he was gone.

My head was spinning none of this made any sense. He seemed so nice but I couldn't shake this feeling that he was the one responsible for me being here. Why was he being so deceitful? I know he is lying I'm just not sure if it's all lies. I needed all the pieces to put it all together.

CHAPTER TEN

Unwanted Protection

I GLANCED OVER at the clock it was twelve fifteen. A little too nice Jenifer said. I looked at her a little confused and asked what do you mean? Nothing she said as she was finishing pushing the medication into my IV. Then she turned out the lights and the last thing I heard was goodnight Elizabeth.

As I began to dream I saw myself lying in a big bed someone was kissing my forehead. I opened my eyes and saw Jay. This time he was smiling at me. He said I'm going to get some breakfast I will be right back. I was stretching and said okay. Then he whispered please don't go anywhere. I said I'm not. As soon as he left I got up and staggered to the bathroom half asleep. I went to the sink and started to wash my face after brushing my teeth. I decided to take a shower.

When I got out I heard a door shut. I quickly put some clothes on and went to see what he brought back. As soon as my eyes locked with his I saw anger flash in his eyes. I wasn't sure what I had done wrong but I started to feel sick. Where do you think you are going he asked? Nowhere I said. I know you aren't dressed like that he said pointedly. I was wearing a white tee and a pair of shorts things that I just wore around the house. But I wasn't about to point that out and start an argument. So I just said of course not.

He said okay come over here and eat. I made my way over to the table he was already sitting down. I grabbed a plate to put my biscuit on. And we both ate in silence he said do you want to watch some television. I said sure and I gathered the plates and rinsed them off before putting them in the dishwasher and made my way into the living room. He was in the bathroom so I grabbed the remote and started looking for something on the television to watch. When he returned he started screaming what did you turn it for. I didn't know you were watching it yet I said.

He started to throw things off of the end table then he walked over a turned the television over. Yelling at the top of his lungs you see what you do bitch. I knew what was coming. I watched myself begging him to calm down telling him that I was sorry and that I loved him. He continued to get louder he was saying you disgust me and that I was a waste of space. That I was lucky to have him. I started to walk out of the room but he threw the remote hitting me in the back of my head. I stopped and turned and asked him why are you doing this? I already knew the answer but I stood there waiting for another excuse. Because you don't love me enough he screamed.

I can go and pay a whore to do things better. You are too sorry to rub my back until I fall asleep at night. How sorry do you have to be I do everything for you he screamed. I screamed back in anger no one is going to rub your back for three and four hours at a time. My hands get tired and I get tired too! He came charging towards me then he grabbed me by the throat until I could no longer breathe. Then he let go but not before hitting me and knocking me unconscious.

I heard radios when I came too like walkie talkies I was in the bed once again. The door was closed but I could hear men talking and Jay saying do I have too wake her. I told you everything was fine they must have heard the radio playing I had it pretty load while I was working out. I heard a man say sir please step away from the door.

The officer entered the bedroom and walked over to the bed. I had the cover over my face. He said ma'am. I said yes. Can you let me see your face? I said do I have too? I have a migraine and the lights make it worse. We got a call about a disturbance from your neighbors is everything okay? Are you okay? Yes, I replied we had the radio up a little loud earlier that's why I have this migraine but everything is fine. Okay ma'am if you need anything all you have to do is call. I laughed and said I promise I don't need any protection everything is fine have a goodnight........

CHAPTER ELEVEN

Feeling Left Out

I AWOKE AND pushed the call bell. Jenifer came in right away. Are you okay she asked? Yes, I am in a little pain though. I knew that I probably should have told her about me having another bad dream but I had a feeling she already knew. Can't sleep either huh she asked? Not really I said. Okay I'll be back with something for both in a minute she said while patting my leg which hurt like hell. But I know she wasn't doing it on purpose.

When she returned she walked straight to the IV and began giving me the medicine. Detective Jones will be here in a few hours to speak with you she said. Did he say what he wanted to talk about I asked? Not really but I got the distinct feeling he was not too happy about your fiancé showing up three weeks after you had been beaten almost to death and then demanding to see you Jenifer said. I was a little shocked by how blunt she was but hey I asked. Besides I guess she had no reason to hold anything back. And as shocked as I was I appreciated her honesty.

That's when I decided to just ask her. Do you think he could have did this to me Jenifer? That's not for me to say Elizabeth. The only thing

I know is that Detective Jones worked very hard to keep him out of this room and away from you she said. Why I asked her? That's something you need to talk to Jones about she said. Why do I feel like everyone knows what is going on but me I asked? Elizabeth we all are just looking out for your best interest she said.

Is he keeping everyone from coming to see me I asked looking her in the eye? He did go as far as to keep all visitors out by getting Dr. Michaelson to put you on the restricted visitors list. Of course Christian did not like it to say the least but if it would have kept your fiancé out he agreed. That meant only the staff and detectives was the only ones who could enter your room without prior authorization. Christian came by to ask how you were tonight but he left fuming. The fact that he couldn't see you but your fiancés lawyer got the department head to change the visitation orders for him really didn't sit well with him to say the least. But that's everything I know she said.

As she turned to leave the room I tried to adjust myself and she saw me wince. Jenifer said I am giving you something else for the pain. I only gave you half a dose earlier in case you needed anything sooner than later. I started to argue but stopped myself. I wasn't going to ask for anything because I didn't want to feel foggy when I spoke with Detective Jones. But it's almost five a.m. and not getting any sleep is beginning to wear on me. At this point I say bring on the fog. Besides my talk with Detective Jones isn't going to be all that pleasant seeing he has decided to make decisions for me.

It seems to me that everyone knows what I need better than me. As I lay here looking out of the window I realized that I haven't had a say so in anything since I got here. I don't get the opportunity to say no to anything. They think they can decide everything for me well I have had enough. I am an amnesia patient. I'm not an infant I'm a grown woman that is being treated like a child by people I don't even know. It's not like I know anyone but they still should ask me damn it! Nope it is not going to be a pleasant conversation at all.

CHAPTER TWELVE

Anger

As I LAID there waiting for the nurse to come back. I was trying to wrap my head around everything that happened tonight. Fiancé really? I can't be engaged especially not to a psychopath. I keep wondering how I ended up here? About all the pain I have endured. And that he may have did this to me. I mean how angry can you get! Then my mind went to the mother that I don't remember. Would I even recognize her? That's when I felt the first of many hot tears streaming down my cheeks.

Jenifer came walking back into my room. When she looked at my face her smile disappeared and was replaced by a look of concern. Are the tears because of your pain or.... Before she could finish her sentence I blurted out I don't even remember my own mothers name! Jenifer made her way over to the bed and hugged me. I probably would have pulled away sooner any other time but right now I needed it.

Jenifer slowly pulled away and asked if there was anything she could do? She even offered to call Detective Jones at five thirty in the morning to ask for my mother's name. That made me smile. I could picture the grumpy Detective having to get up at that time in the morning just for my mother's name. I giggled a little thinking this is one brave girl. But right after I giggled I felt an explosion of pain running through my rib cage.

That's when Jenifer began pushing the medication into the IV. It wasn't long before my whole body started to relax as the pain began to ease. At that moment I realized how exhausted I was. I fell asleep only a few moments after Jenifer had left the room. I must have begun to dream again it was like seeing yourself and everything around you through someone else's eyes. This dream was like little flashes of different moments. The first moment I saw myself running towards a door. When I reached out to open the door I felt someone wrapping my hair around their hand and pulling me back away from the door. I screamed from the pain falling to the floor as he continued to drag me further away from the door.

I kicked him in the shin I couldn't see his face but I knew who it was. He released me for a second and he began to curse. I wasted no time I began to get up so I could run but he grabbed my foot. I started kicking franticly I landed one to his face. I was able to get up and run for the door. I opened the door only to feel the same pain as before. I screamed in agony as I was pulled once more through the doorway. I was praying that someone would see or hear me and call for help but no one ever did.

Then I saw Jay standing over me. He was standing there looking at me with more anger and hatred than I ever thought possible. He was screaming, you think you can just leave me you stupid bitch over and over again. Each time he would scream I prepared for another blow. As they continued to rain down on me until I lost consciousness.

The next flash or memory was different he wasn't angry. He was calm and even sweet. I was in bed and he was sitting on the side of the bed telling me how much he loved me as he kissed my forehead. He asked if I needed anything. Then began to tell me how sorry he was. That's when I woke up but I wasn't screaming or crying even though I didn't know what scared me the most his angry side or the sweet loving one.

The more I thought about all of these nightmares or memories the angrier I became. I was no longer frightened. All of my fear had turned into anger. I can't see how I could ever love a monster. But I couldn't stay in denial. I knew these dreams weren't dreams at all. They were memories my memories of Jay and I. He did this to me and I was determined to find out why and make him pay.

CHAPTER THIRTEEN

Learning to Trust

GOOD MORNING ELIZABETH, Dr. Michaelson said as he was walking through the door. Ughh, Yeah I guess I replied. He made his way over to my bedside. How are you today he asked? Are you sure you really want to know I asked hoping he would say no? It isn't top secret is it? Let me guess if you tell me you have to kill me he said with a huge smile on his face. And if I wasn't dealing with no sleep and an extreme amount of pain right now. I would have found it amusing but right now it's just aggravating.

So I just smiled and said I'm exhausted, in pain and I have a massive headache. Oh and I'm feeling really irritable right about now. He just continued smiling. And just that alone was annoying right now. All of this is to be expected Elizabeth, after the night that you have had he said. Just rest today Rhonda will be in shortly with your medication hopefully that will help with the pain and headache. He said but the only thing I can subscribe for exhaustion is rest. I smiled and said okay I will try he turned and disappeared into the hallway.

I sat there trying to make sense of it all but the more I thought about everything the less sense any of it made. I feel so helpless, ashamed, and afraid. But most of all I feel angry. I am angry with myself for letting him do this to me. I picked up the mirror on the bedside table. I sat there staring at my still purple eyes and some of the other bruises marring my face. I began to cry how could I be in this situation? An even better question is how am I going to get out of it.

I don't understand why if he is the one who did this? Why would he even claim to know me? He's lying but I don't know why or what about? And I don't know who I can trust because if I tell anyone I know it was him. I will never get the answers I need. Good morning, Rhonda said bringing me back into the room and pulling me away from my thoughts. Good morning, I mumbled back.

I understand you have had an eventful night she said as she walked over to the IV. Don't worry she smiled I am going to give you your medication but I am under strict orders to make sure no one bothers you including myself she giggled. Dr. Wilcox will be in soon but after that you can get some much needed rest.

Dr. Michaelson said you would be here today did you enjoy your day off I asked? She blushed every time I said anything about Dr. Michaelson mentioning her. It was kind of cute the way the two of them acted especially when they were in the same room. They both blushed so much it looked like those blinking red Christmas lights.

She said yes I was able to catch up on some reading she said. That was something Rhonda and I had in common we both loved to read. Just last week she asked me if I liked to read and when I told her yes she brought me five books the next day. Well maybe more like novels. Well that's good I said. She nodded and smiled as she continued giving me my medications.

When she was done I asked if she would bring my things I used to wash up and brush my teeth with and a clean gown if she didn't mind helping me to change afterwards? Of course she replied then she hurried back into the hallway before I could even say thank you.

She came back a few minutes later carrying a large basin, a few washcloths, two towels and a clean gown. When I got a closer look at the basin there was a tooth brush, tooth paste, soap, shampoo, and lotion. I knew I was going to sleep better this was the closest thing to a bath I have had in weeks. I know right I feel down right grimy but I had to wait for Dr. Michaelson to okay it because of my sutures.

I told Rhonda thank you. She said I will be assisting you. There is no need for you to do that I told her. She said you aren't able to get up yet and you'll need water besides Doctors orders. I knew there was no need in arguing they always won. So I just smiled and nodded my head yes in agreement.

Then another young girl came in carrying sheets, pillow cases and another blanket. I asked how are you going to make the bed if I can't get up? Her eyes narrowed a little then she said we will manage and smiled. When everything was done I felt like a new person well except for the pain that is. They had me moving all over the place and of course that didn't help with the pain any. But never the less I was grateful.

They lifted my broken leg to elevate it with some pillows. I moaned a little and Rhonda gave me that it's medication time look. I told her I was fine but she said that it was time. I looked at the clock and was shocked to see that three hours had passed since the last time she had given me anything. I nodded my head yes. I will be right back she said.

The other girl helping her had just finished cleaning and putting everything away when Rhonda came back and started giving me the medication. The lady helping had left the room when I made the decision to talk to Rhonda about my visitor from last night. She stayed and listened while I continued telling her how afraid I was of him and how I wasn't sure why. When I was done she looked at me and said Elizabeth you really should talk to Dr. Wilcox about how you are feeling.

Yes, I should but I don't trust him I thought to myself. Then I smiled and said I will thank you for listening. She smiled but her smile didn't reach her eyes when she spoke this time saying I know sometimes it's hard to trust others. But you will learn in time to trust again. She came over and gave me a quick hug before she shut my door she said don't worry my lips are sealed. And I sat there thinking I just did trust someone her. I wasn't sure when it happened but I had come to trust Rhonda.

CHAPTER FOURTEEN

Breakdown

I THOUGHT I would stop back in to see how your pain is Dr. Michaelson said. I had been looking out the window and I didn't even hear him come in. I am actually in a tremendous amount of pain I said. He came closer and said where is your pain he asked? I had been having pain in my right side since this morning but it has gotten worse.

Suddenly the pain doubled me over and I threw up all over poor Dr. Michaelson. Lay back he said after going to the sink to wash up. Then he walked over to where I was lying. He began pushing on my stomach. It didn't hurt until he pushed in on my lower right side. That's when I let out a scream from the pain.

He hit the call bell. Rhonda came running in I didn't even notice how they were acting I was in so much pain. But when I looked up and saw their faces I knew something was wrong. Dr. Michaelson said I am going to change and come right back Elizabeth. I couldn't speak the pain was excruciating. I was scared to even move but I managed to nod my head letting him know I would be okay. He glanced at Rhonda and said medication and have the ultra sound set up and ready for when I return. Rhonda and Dr. Michaelson headed out into the hall.

Rhonda was the first to return with medication. She began pushing it in to the IV. I fell unconscious before she had even finished. I awoke in a different room there was no one there but I saw people walking past the room I was in. I was groggy and I still was having a hard time keeping my eyes open. I closed my eyes only for what seemed like a few moments that's when I heard Dr. Michaelson. Elizabeth can you hear me he asked?

I opened my eyes and said what happened? He looked at me with a kind of sadness in his eyes. That's when I prepared myself for bad news. You had a miscarriage he almost whispered. What but I wasn't pregnant you would have known. Right you would have known I yelled. No when you came in you weren't far enough along and we couldn't have known. I am so sorry Elizabeth he said.

Can I have some time to myself please I asked? Of course he said as he turned to leave. I wasn't really sure what I felt I was sad for the life that was lost for my...my ...child. But I was also angry because this was Jays doing. That's when I felt this odd sense of relief about not having his child. Then came the guilt for feeling the relief. That's when I cried. That went on for two days. Then I had no more tears just this feeling of complete emptiness.

I began to shut down completely. I refused to see Dr. Wilcox. I only gave the nurses and doctor straight to the point answers nothing more nothing less. I just laid there staring out the window not really thinking about anything it was like being in a constant daze. I felt as if the emptiness had swallowed me whole. I signed the paper Jones had wanted saying that I didn't want any visitors. That didn't stop Christian or Jay from coming by not that Jay was concerned about anyone but himself. They didn't know the reason for me not wanting visitors. Only that I didn't want any visitors. Christian however would stop by and ask Rhonda how I was and give her messages for me.

But none of that mattered to me. I just couldn't be around anyone even if that meant everyone around me thinking I have had a complete breakdown. I only wanted two things to sleep and to be completely alone...

CHAPTER FIFTEEN

Time to Heal

IT HAS BEEN two weeks so I decided it was time to lift the visitation ban yesterday. I still don't feel like myself but I knew that I couldn't continue to avoid my problems. I have been here six weeks now I have healed a lot physically but there is still so much more I need to know if I am going to continue healing mentally. I had to talk with Detective Jones today. I was supposed to speak with him the day that I had the miscarriage and I have been putting it off since.

So I had Rhonda contact him yesterday afternoon to arrange a meeting with him as soon as possible. She said he said he would be here today at four pm. She also said that he seemed eager to meet with me also. I guess we will see how everything goes.

Elizabeth, Dr. Wilcox said as he walked straight to the bed side chair and sat down. It's been a while. Yeah I guess it has I replied. So how have you been he asked? There it was the question I had been trying to avoid because I have no answer. I'm not really sure I said. He only nodded looking at his clipboard. I hadn't seen Dr. Wilcox in a while. But not much had changed with the shrink most of the time he just sits in the same chair nodding his head and writing things down on the clipboard rarely making eye contact.

I'm not sure what I used to do for a living but I know what I should be doing. He reminds me of one of those bobble heads that sits on the dashboard of someone's car. Elizabeth? Yes, I answered looking completely confused. I asked you what you weren't sure about he said? Oh sorry I didn't hear you I said. I'm not sure how I feel about anything. I just feel empty. You are grieving so many things he said. You have lost so much Elizabeth. First you lost your independence then your identity and who you are as a person. And now with this child you are dealing with more than one person should have to ever endure in a lifetime. And it will take time for you to heal. But I will tell you that you are one of the strongest women I have ever met. And if anyone can overcome all these things my money is on you.

I want you to use the next few days to think about what all you have lost and how you are going to deal with these things. I am going out of town for a few days but when I get back we will start working on the healing process. I have already began healing I said. He looked up from his clipboard and said yes but sometimes things appear normal on the outside even though there may be a storm brewing on the inside.

I understand that I said but I think it will be a very long time for this storm to pass. He nodded and smiled. I will be back in two days and we can see what the forecast is then. He stood and walked into the hallway. I may never heal completely I thought as I watched him walk out of the room.

Fifteen minutes after Dr. Wilcox left Dr. Michaelson walked through the door. How are you today he asked? A little sore but other than that I'm fine I said. How's the ankles and leg? That's what's sore I said. It will get better. Yeah if you say so Doc. The longer you do the physical therapy you will start to see a difference he said.

Of course I wasn't buying that. I have been doing physical therapy for a week now and all I felt so far was pain and embarrassment. No one tells you that after being laid up for six weeks with a few broken bones you are going to walk like a baby giraffe taking its first steps. Oh the stories I bet these people tell when they get home at night.

Just hang in there you are making remarkable progress. We both sat there in silence for a moment before he began to speak again. I realize this all must be hard for you. But we truly do care about you and your wellbeing. We all realize that you have had so much taken from you. I really don't want you to feel pushed to do anything. Or that you do not have a say in your treatment.

But I also want you to realize this physical therapy is one of the most important thing for you right now. It is the only thing you can do to help yourself to get back to the way you were before. I looked down at the floor like a little kid after a speech from a parent. I understand I said. Good, I will see you again in the morning he said as he left the room.

CHAPTER SIXTEEN

More Questions

AFTER DR. MICHAELSON had stepped into the hallway I could hear him speaking with the nurse. But I couldn't really make out what they were saying. My right eardrum had somehow been ruptured and I still had no hearing in that ear. The doctor says that my hearing will come back but I am not so sure he is right. And bad hearing is definitely not what I need right now. It makes it very hard to eavesdrop. As I sat there trying to make out what was being said I heard another male voice.

Then was a knock at my door. I yelled out come in. When the door opened I saw Detective Jones. He was a tall slender man with brown hair and dark brown eyes. He always had dark circles under his eyes from lack of sleep I suppose. And he was wearing all black. My stomach was suddenly in knots. Don't get me wrong I was glad to finally see him but I knew nothing that he was going to tell me could possibly be good. He walked straight in and shook my hand. Which shouldn't be awkward but it was a little. I mean it's not the first time we have met. Even though it has been a while but he always introduces himself and tells me everything except the size of his underwear. Not that I want to know and that's my point I don't need to know everything.

Maybe it's just me but at this point I feel as if we could skip the formalities. He asked if I minded if he sat so we could talk I said yes even though he was already sitting. I am sorry for your loss Elizabeth. How did you know I bit out? They had to tell me I thought you knew? This changes some things about the case. Like what I asked? Well first off whoever gets charged in your case will be charged with attempted murder and first degree murder.

As I sat there waiting for my brain to wrap around what he just said I almost started to cry I had not thought about that at all. He cleared his throat and said I realize how hard this must be for you but I need to ask you some more questions about Jason or Jay as you call him. I just nodded letting him know it was okay. First did either of you know you were pregnant? No I don't think so but I don't really remember everything either.

You still don't remember who did this to you? No.... But I.... What is it he asked? I can't prove it but I know he did this. How he asked? Because my dreams or memories in all of them he was abusive and angry. I understand but I have to have more to go on than your dreams to arrest him. I know I said. But that's all I have.

Don't worry I have a friend who is a private investigator and he is working with me to find out all I can about him. We will get something. Besides I knew when I met him that something was way off he said. By the way I hope you're not still upset that I cut off your visitation to try to keep him away he asked? I sat there nodding no but I was thinking hell yes I was still upset I was the one who should have made that decision. But I kept nodding my head willing him to continue. I guess I did learn a few things from good old DR. Bobble head. I smiled trying to hold back the laughter from picturing Dr. Wilcox's head bobbing around.

But then I realized Detective Jones hadn't continued. He sat there watching me. So I sat straight up and told myself to hold it together. I knew that lack of sleep was catching up with me. Elizabeth, Elizabeth, I heard Jones saying pulling me away from my thoughts. Oh yeah sorry I was thinking. He gave me a look and raised his eyebrows and then picked back up right where he left off saying, I am sorry that I stopped Christian from visiting. He continued explaining, if I had let Christian in then that would have made it easier for Jason's lawyer to get him in sooner. And don't worry I explained everything too Christian and he agreed that it would be for the best if we didn't make it easier for Jason to get to you.

My eyebrow shot up I was feeling confused but curious to know where this was going. What exactly do you mean by get to me? Okay I was hoping to tell you these things slowly as your memory had progressed a little more but I think you know Jay is our primary suspect. Really our only suspect he said. Then his cell phone started ringing he pulled it away from the clip on his pocket and said I have to take this. He got up and walked to the doorway and answered the phone.

Once he was done and hung up he walked back over to my bedside this time he didn't sit down he continued to stand there as he began talking once more. That was the Private Detective he wants to meet up tonight he says he has information about Jay. Can we meet again tomorrow at the same time and I will fill you in on the details then. I said sure. Elizabeth. I said yes. We will get him and you will get the closure you need to heal. Thank you I said softly as he was leaving the room.

CHAPTER SEVENTEEN

Small steps toward happiness

I LOOKED UP to see Christian walking through the door all I could see was his gorgeous smile my heart melted. That's when I realized how much I missed him. Hey stranger he said. I don't know why but when I said hello back it was almost a whisper. I knew I had a good reason for keeping everyone away. I needed the time to myself but I still felt a little guilty for keeping Christian away. He had been nothing but supportive through all of this and he just met me six weeks ago.

He came over and sat on the edge of my bed. How have you been he asked? I said okay. I knew that he knew different but I was sure he asked to be polite. How have you been I asked? I have been horrible. Why I asked? Because my best friend wasn't talking to me he said with a sly grin. They don't sound like a very good friend to me I said smiling. He said well I kind of really like her he said.

I felt a rush of heat flooding my cheeks. No response he asked. All I could manage to do was clear my throat. Okay then so I hear you can walk he said giving me a light punch in the arm. OUCH I said trying to contain my smile! I'm sorry he said then I burst out in a fit of laughter. I'm kidding and yes I can walk it's not pretty but I'm able to get where I am going.

Good cause I have a surprise for you tomorrow. What is it I asked? I guess you'll just have to wait and see he said. That's not fair I said poking out my bottom lip. You of all people should know life's not fair Elizabeth. And you also should know that poking your lip out like that could be dangerous. Just what are you saying you know I'm engaged I asked? First of all, your engaged to a total psychopath. And secondly I am saying unless you want me to kiss you quit teasing me with your lips.

When did you become so pushy I asked? When I realized you were with a total dick and that I am so much better for you. You seem awfully sure of yourself I said. Well I figure it like this I helped save your life he almost took it I think that puts me in the lead. This isn't a contest Christian I said. No it's not he said and gave me a half smile. Besides I know your joking I said. His eyebrows furrowed together. Then he just shrugged his shoulders as if to say whatever.

That's when I decided it was time to ask him. Why did you continue to come see me after you ummm...? Saved me. I mean do you keep visiting a lot of people after you bring them in. He looked like he was deep in thought. No he said I have never visited anyone else he said. Really I said. Yes, really. Oh so why me then I asked. I looked down when I asked because I didn't want him to see my heat flushed cheeks. I don't really know. At first I was curious to see if you would make it. Then you did and I thought this girl is tough. I was just really curious about you. And once I got to know you some the more I wanted to know. Before I knew it we were friends.

My heart sank a little. He said exactly what I thought he would say but it wasn't what I wanted to hear. And even though it hurt and I was expecting it I felt a little angry at him I wasn't sure why but I was. So what time are you coming by tomorrow a little after twelve. Oh I said. What's wrong? Nothing it's just that Detective Jones will be coming by about the same time to discuss some new information I said. That's not a problem I have tomorrow off and we can work around it. I can find something to do while you two talk he said. Well I was hoping maybe you would be here with me. He smiled that sweet sexy smile that always made my heart melt. Of course I will whatever makes you happy he said.

CHAPTER EIGHTEEN

Unwanted Visitor

AFTER CHRISTIAN LEFT I went to physical therapy then I came back to my room and took a nap. I woke just in time for dinner which I ate. I had gotten used to the hospital food but being used to it and liking it was two different things. But a girl has to eat. There was a knock on my door but before I could say anything I looked up and Jay was walking in.

How are you Elizabeth? I'm great can't you tell I snapped. Well someone's in a mood he said smiling which made me want to throw up. Why are you here I asked? Well I figured since your other boyfriend came by then surely you would want to see your fiancé. I don't have another boyfriend. Also I don't believe you can be engaged to someone you can't remember. Besides I don't even like you.

That's what you said the first day we met. Well there is your sign I said. He said you're not even giving me a chance. And why are you so angry with me he asked? Maybe because you're a murdering piece of crap to put it nicely I thought to myself. I guess you just bring out the best in me I said. Well I'll keep that in mind. I brought you something.

I don't want it I said looking away from him. You don't even know what it is.

And I don't need to know I spat out. Well at least look at it before you say you don't want it. Fine I said what is it. He walked over to me and got down on his knees and said would you be my wife again. Are you kidding me you really are crazy aren't you I said. I know nothing about you and what I do know I don't like! What is it that you think you don't like he asked?

Well you're a liar for one I said. What have I lied to you about? Uh well let's see I was supposed to meet my mom she was on a plane here four weeks ago. That's the longest plane ride in history I said trying not to raise my voice. I don't know what happened to that she hasn't called me since. And you may not remember but your family never was dependable and frankly they never gave a shit! I was the only one you could ever depend on he yelled.

You need to lower your voice and I don't believe you I said. I love you he said but if you're not careful you are going to lose the only person you've got. You are not the only person I can depend on even though I am sure that's what you would like me to believe I yelled. That's when he really got angry and said I don't know why I even bothered. Bothered what I asked?

Before he could answer Jenifer my night shift nurse came in. What is all the noise in here is everything alright Elizabeth? Before I could speak Jay began speaking for me. Everything is fine he said. She stood there looking between the two of us. Well I'm sorry to say but visiting hours are over and it is time for me to get Elizabeth's sleep meds. And she needs her rest.

He looked at me and smiled and said I guess I will see you tomorrow dear. My skin began to crawl but I wasn't going to allow him to see that he was affecting me in any way. I nodded and said goodnight. As soon as he left the room Jenifer said who is that again? My fiancé I said. Oh she said. I said it's okay I really don't know him or like him. She smiled and said I can't blame you he gives me the creeps. Me too....

Chapter Nineteen

Discovery

WHEN I WOKE the next morning it was six a.m. I got up and showered. Once I was finished and dressed I went back to bed and waited for breakfast too come. It came at seven thirty. I ate brushed my teeth. I was nervous today was possibly the day I would get some answers. And Christian was going to surprise me with god knows what. I had all this energy and no way of getting rid of it.

Hi Elizabeth, I heard someone say I turned and looked to see Dr. Michaelson standing inside the doorway. Hi I replied. How are you doing today? I'm good I said. Well I have some news that will make your day even better. What's that I asked? No physical therapy today. Why what's up? It's everyone they are having workshops today and tomorrow for every department. I guess your right it does make the day just a little better I said as I giggled.

He lifted an eyebrow just a little better huh he said smiling. Are you sure you are alright he asked? Yeah I just have a lot on my mind. Okay I guess I will take your word for it he said smiling. Then Rhonda walked in and his attention immediately turned to her as he watched her moving with purpose around the room. How are you today Rhonda

Dr. Michaelson asked never taking his eyes off of her? I'm doing fine hope you are as well Rhonda responded in a softer voice than usual. I watched them wondering if he noticed how her face had flushed every time he was in the same room. He nodded and said I will see you both later. Rhonda simply said see you later never making eye contact.

A few moments after Dr. Michaelson had left the room Dr. Wilcox arrived. Good morning ladies he said as he made his way over to the chair he always sat in. How are you today Elizabeth he asked? I'm angry. I guess it caught him off guard because he looked up from his clipboard. About what he asked? I'm angry at Jay I said. That's very understandable. I know but I get angry just looking at him. Do you want to harm him? Oh hell I know where this is going no but I'm mad. I don't want to be in the same room with him. Well you have the right to not see him or talk to him he said. I know I replied. Is there anything else bothering you? Not really well this is an easy fix you can keep him from seeing you he said.

Yes, your right I know what I need to do I said quietly. Well how are the dreams. You mean memories I said pointedly. So you are sure that's what they are? Yes, I'm pretty sure it's just complicated I don't want to make any accusations until I am one hundred percent sure though I said. I would be very cautious myself he said glancing up from his clip board just don't begin to doubt the importance of these dreams you are having. I don't I said. He glanced at the clock which made me look too it had been an hour that's the longest we have ever talked. He looked back at me and said times up we will have to pick up where we left off tomorrow. Then he stood up and said so tomorrow same place same time and smiled. And he left my room disappearing into the hall way.

I sat there watching the clock waiting for Christian or Detective Jones to show up. Rhonda came in right before lunch with my medications.

She said Detective Jones wanted me to let you know that he was on his way. Okay, have you heard from Christian? She smiled and said I think he may be around here somewhere. Good I said he was supposed to be here when Jones arrived. No worries Elizabeth if Christian said he will be here he will he's a very dependable person she said.

The way she said it made me a little curious about how she knew this? So I asked her how long have you known Christian? We have worked together for a long time now but he is my brother. She asked are you alright? That's when I realized I was just sitting there like a retard with my mouth gaping wide open. Yes, I said I didn't realize...I trailed off. She said I didn't mention it before because it wasn't relevant. And now I asked? Well now it's obvious my brother has feelings for you and I don't think he would mind me telling you. How do you feel about that I asked her? I am happy for him and you she said with a smile. Good I said with the same goofy grin on my face that I have when I see her brother.

Rhonda came over and hugged me and said see you later. Then she left. I laid down and five minutes later I heard a knock on my door. I sat up and seen Christian standing there smiling at me. So I hear you met my sister I hope you won't hold it against me. Very funny I said. So are you ready for your surprise he asked with a playful look on his face. Sure I said. He walked out of the room and was carrying a shopping bag in one hand and a picnic basket in the other.

What's all this? Well it's a picnic basket he said and laughed. I know that but what are we going to do have a picnic in my room? No silly outside he said. I don't think they are going to... Before I could finish my sentence he interrupted me saying I already have permission. How? I am a paramedic you know. I just had to agree to assume responsibility if anything was to happen he said with a sly grin. I can't go outside in this hospital gown people will think I escaped from the mental ward I said frowning. There are clothes that will fit you in the bag.

So you thought of everything huh? Well with some help from my sister you just met I'm not very good at picking out women's clothing and she knew what size you wore he said. About that why did you never mention that Rhonda was your sister? Well it was kind of weird that I kept visiting and even though her taking care of you was a coincidence. I figured you might think it was a little creepy he said as he sat in the chair beside my bed squirming around a little as he spoke. I laughed a little and then asked if I could go try on the clothes he smiled and said anything you want.

By the time I came out of the bathroom after changing I realized I didn't have any shoes. At that same moment Rhonda came in holding a pair of brand new tennis shoes. I bit back tears and told them both thank you so much. She jokingly said no problem I like having my brother owing me a favors. He just rolled his eyes. Then there was a knock on the door we all turned to see who it was.

Jones was standing there looking like a deer caught in headlights. He cleared his throat and said am I interrupting something. That's when Rhonda spoke up and said I was just leaving and then left the room. I turned to Jones and said Christian will be staying. Jones just nodded and closed the door. He made his way to the other chair. Once he was settled he looked at me and said are you ready to hear what I found out. I said I've been ready.

That's when he began by telling me that he met with his private investigator yesterday and that I needed to prepare myself for what he had discovered about Jay and what I was about to hear....

CHAPTER TWENTY

There is a storm coming

JONES SAID HE has done this before not to the extent that he beat you but we spoke with a few women he dated before you and even some while he was with you. And he has always been abusive toward women even his own mother. So he did do this to me I said. Yes, I believe so but we have to prove it before we can charge him. And he can't know that we suspect him either.

Why? Because he has done this before and gotten away with this so many times we dug a little deeper to see how. How did he keep getting away with this and found that his father is high up in the Justice department and has called in many favor's? So we need to keep this quiet and let him think he has everything under control until we have enough evidence to charge him.

He has also escalated with his abusive behavior and I am worried that he may go as far as to cover up what he has done he said looking at me with a look of concern. Are you saying he might try to kill her Christian spat out? Yes, that is exactly what I am saying. How long do I have to keep living in fear I asked?

As long as it takes he replied. Look I am working as hard as I can I want him locked away just as much as you do. But it's not your life on the line Jones Christian said. I realize this Jones snapped back. He is smart and manipulative he knows what he is doing he thinks ahead and that with his connections make him very dangerous. He maneuvers people around like chess pieces and his confidence is at and all time high because no one has ever made anything he has been charged with stick.

We are hoping that will be his undoing. He was high in the military he made a career out of it. That is years and years of training from breaking people down and controlling them to strategizing and staying one step ahead of everyone. But we can use some of this to our advantage and we will. Right now I need you to be patient Elizabeth he said.

What choice do I have? You don't he said. Okay well we will do what we have to do I said. Christian said how do you plan on protecting her from this psychopath. Beginning tomorrow morning we will have an undercover officer working on the floor. This way he has no idea what is going on. He will not hurt you ever again Jones said. Don't make promises you can't keep Jones Christian said. Jones stood and said I will be back to speak with you when I have anything new. Then without another word he left the room.

Are you okay Christian asked? Yes. Are you sure do you still want to go for a picnic because we can go another time if you're not up to it he asked? No we are going I refuse to let him have any more control over my life he has taken enough I said in a determined tone. Okay then are you ready beautiful he said making me blush. Whenever you're ready handsome I answered back.

Once we got outside he told me to follow him as he walked behind the hospital. We finally stopped in a beautiful area with benches and flowers of all colors surrounding us. There were trees everywhere which I was thankful for their shade. I broke the silence and said this place is beautiful. Well it's what I had to work with since they wouldn't let us leave the property he smiled and said. It is perfect I told him. Well I am glad you like it he replied as he spread a blanket on the ground. Thank you I said. He just smiled and said please sit. I sat down on the blanket and felt the warmth on my skin. What made you do this I said? I see the way you look out the window I could tell how much you wanted to go outside. So are you ready to chow down. Oh yeah I said laughing at how playful he was. I happen to look up as he was getting the food out of the basket. I saw a figure standing a few yards away behind a big oak tree. I asked Christian did he see them? And before I knew what he was doing he started walking towards the person standing by the tree. Suddenly the person took off running with Christian chasing after them.

I couldn't tell if it was a man or a woman but they had on sweats and a hoodie which was unusual for as hot as it was. When Christian returned he said lunch has been cut short I am sorry Elizabeth but we need to get back. Sensing the tightness in his voice I began helping to pack everything back up. I waited until we were back in my room and asked was it him? I don't know he had a hoodie on and I couldn't see his face but if I had to guess it probably was him. Why would anyone else run.

He picked up the phone and dialed a number. Yes, he said could you connect me with Detective Jones please. I sat there listening to the conversation. I was not scared but I was angry. My anger for this man had made it to another level. I was tired of his games. I wanted my life back and him out of it. Christian hung up the phone sat down on the edge of my bed and was apologizing. You have no reason to apologize I said. He made a face and said I wish he would just...

He didn't finish the sentence he just sat there staring out of my window. I am going to tell him tonight that I know it was him and that he needs to leave me alone forever I said. You know that you can't do that Elizabeth. You heard what Jones said. It could just make things worse he said. I knew that he was probably right but it wasn't what I wanted to hear right now and I started to tell him so but I thought better of it. I needed all the friends I could get right now. So far Jones had been unsuccessful in contacting my family. But he said he would keep trying.

CHAPTER TWENTY-ONE

Taken

IT WAS SEVEN p.m. and Christian had left an hour ago after I had agreed to not say anything to Jay to tip him off or make him mad. I didn't take the time to explain that if I was nice to Jay now he would think something was up. I was writing in my Journal when Jenifer walked in it was shift change. I'm giving your medication early tonight if you need anything you will have to hit the call bell tonight she said as she was rushing around the room. What's up I asked? There will only be two people on the floor tonight because of this mandatory workshop she explained.

And not to mention the storm coming and they say we are going to lose power she said. She stopped for a moment and smiled. Do you need anything before I go she asked? No I will be fine I replied. Okay then I will see you later on tonight and remember if you need anything use the call bell. Then she disappeared into the hallway.

I was waiting on them to bring my dinner trey when I saw Jay standing in the doorway. He was holding a bouquet of flowers and smiling he walked over to the chair and sat down. Jay sat there in silence looking at me. He finally spoke asking how was your day my dear Lizzy?

Suddenly a sick feeling washed over me as I thought about the man Christian had chased away earlier that day.

It was uneventful I answered hoping that he would continue the conversation without wanting me to elaborate any farther. So he said no special outings today? That's when I realized he was playing with me he knew exactly what I did today because he was there. Was that you today out by the tree Jay? Because if so that's called stalking I said.

Well that's interesting. So let me get this right he said smugly. I happened to be on my way to visit my fiancé and happened to see her having lunch with another man. Who by the way also has been coming to visit every day hmmm he said while pretending to scratch his head. I think most people would agree that it's not stalking if your fiancé is a whore and she's cheating on you he said with his face flushed and his nostrils beginning to flare. It was the same look he had in my nightmares. I pushed away the nauseating feeling I had. Are you kidding me cheating? Cheating I said again raising my voice.

I don't even know you. You are not my fiancé anymore. I want you to leave and never come back I yelled. Oh I am going to leave but I am not leaving you here alone. You are mine you don't tell someone you love them and just change your mind because you want to move on with another guy someone needs to show you the damage you do to others because you're a selfish bitch. You are nothing I mean who do you think you are? You are disgusting you were lucky to have me he screamed.

I could see the lightning and hear the thunder was getting worse I seen the rain pouring out the window. I looked back at Jay. Please leave I begged with tears flowing down my face just as fast as the rain falling outside my window. Leave he said through gritted teeth as he threw the flowers hitting me in my face. I picked up the flowers and threw them into the floor. He was standing over me when he spat in my face and then called me a worthless whore. Then suddenly the lights went out I could hear confusion in the hallway. He had started pacing back and forth but had stopped and walked over to me and grabbing my arm saying get up bitch. No I said as he started to drag me out of the bed.

That's when I saw the gun his shirt had raised just enough for me to see it in the back of his pants. I knew that if I didn't do what he asked he may decide to use the gun and others could possibly be hurt. I took a deep breath and stood as he pushed me into the hallway where there were people everywhere. I was praying that someone would see us and stop us. But no one did that's when I realized no one would we just looked like a couple leaving the hospital because I never changed back into the hospital gown. Once we were out of the hospital he walked me to a silver truck in the front of the hospital parking lot. It had cooled down a lot since earlier that day. The rain was pouring so hard that you almost couldn't see right in front of you.

Where are you taking me? Shut up he said opening the door to the truck and looking around the parking lot nervously. I climbed into the silver truck and put my seat belt on and laughed thinking I've been taken from the hospital by the monster who put me there. I am not sure why I thought the seat belt was going to help keep me safe. What are you laughing at he asked me? Irony I replied. Shut up he yelled. Now what are you planning on doing hiding me away forever?

That's funny you think I care enough to keep you around forever. Why would I keep you around a dog is more loyal than you and prettier too he said laughing? Asshole I said. He grabbed me by the hair put one arm through the steering wheel so that my head was down underneath

CHAPTER TWENTY-TWO

The Blame Game

J ENIFER HAD JUST gotten back on the floor. She got the med cart and started filling it with medication it was five thirty she always tried to have all of her medications handed out by six fifteen. It was important to keep her schedule so she would be finished with everything before shift change. And she was already behind due to the workshop she had to go to earlier.

By the time Jenifer made her way to room two sixteen it was six am. She knocked on the closed door before opening it. She looked around but the patient was not in the room. She glanced over to the bathroom door it was closed she smiled and took a sigh of relief. Elizabeth she said loudly so she could hear her through the bathroom door. I am going to leave your meds on the table take them when you get out okay because I am running behind. I will be back before shift change.

Jenifer knew she could get in trouble for not watching a patient take their medication. And if it had been a normal patient she would have never left the medication like that but Elizabeth has been here so long she knows just as much about the routine as she did. And she never had a problem with Elizabeth taking her medications. No it would be fine she thought to herself.

It was five minutes before shift change and Jenifer decided she better go make sure Elizabeth had taken her meds. When she walked in the door she saw the cup with the medication still sitting where she had left it. She walked over and seen the medicine still in the cup. She turned and walked over to the bathroom door and began knocking there was no answer. So she said I'm coming in. Again no response she swung open the door. Elizabeth was gone... Jenifer's heart sank and then started to beat rapidly. Oh god what have I done she said to herself. She ran out of the room towards the nurse's station where she saw Rhonda clocking in.

Rhonda looked up from the computer where she had clocked in to see Jenifer coming out of Elizabeth's room in a panic. What's wrong Jenifer? Jenifer burst into tears. Jenifer was trying to talk but Rhonda couldn't understand what she was saying because of her crying had turned into a full blown fit. So Rhonda took off running to Elizabeth's room when she had gotten the she realized Elizabeth was gone.

Rhonda ran back to Jenifer. How long has she been gone she asked Jenifer? I... I... don't know she managed to answer. We had the workshop and when I got back the bathroom door was closed. I thought she was in the bathroom. Rhonda immediately walked over to the phone and dialed Detective Jones. Jones you need to get here right away it's Elizabeth she's missing. She heard him spout out a few obscenities before hanging up the phone.

Lock down the floor she shouted a patient is missing. Everyone began running around doing head counts to make sure no one else was missing. Jenifer ran closing off all of the entrances and exits. People would have to be buzzed in and out. Rhonda sat there with a panicked look of her own. Shit Christian... she whispered to herself.

Rhonda hesitated for a moment before deciding to pick up the phone and call her brother. Christian answered after the second ring he had seen the caller identification and knew it was his sister. He also knew that his sister never called from work. He answered the phone with his heart racing preparing himself for whatever he was about to hear.

After his sister told him that Elizabeth was missing he didn't wait for her to finish before hanging up the phone. Christian grabbed his car keys and ran out the door of his condo hopped into his cherry red Jeep and took off for the hospital. As he drove down the road praying that Elizabeth was okay. He was in love with this woman even if she didn't realize it. He had fell in love with this beautiful damaged woman he knew he loved her after watching her fight so hard for her life. And as he drove down the highway all he could think was I should have told her that I loved her.

Once he arrived at the hospital and made it to the floor that Elizabeth had been taken from he saw Jenifer, Rhonda, and Jones were standing in front of Elizabeth's room. Which Jones already had taped off. Rhonda looked up and met Christians gaze and ran over to hug her brother as Jones continued to question Jenifer. How did this happen Christian asked pulling away from his sister? I honestly don't know myself. She was already gone when I arrived for my shift this morning. After she said that Christian made a bee line for Jenifer and Jones before Rhonda could object.

What the hell is going on Jones? And please tell me how a nurse doesn't know when someone kidnaps their patient? Go to hell Christian Jenifer said and stormed off. Christian we don't know that she has been kidnapped Jones said. Christian was pacing and stopped and gave Jones a long hard look and said you're kidding right? Jones said I have someone checking the footage from the cameras here and in the parking lot as soon as we know something bad has happened I would like to try to stay positive. It's not helping anyone to blame someone or throw around accusations....

Chapter Twenty-Three

Waking in Captivity

I woke in a small room about the size of a bathroom. There was just enough room for the bed. At the end of the bed there wasn't even room to put your feet down. There was a nightstand with an old television sitting on top taking up any extra space. I got off of the bed and looked to the left there was at least a bathroom even if it was the size of a broom closet. The room looked old and filthy definitely not the type of place anyone would want to be. I walked to the door it was unlocked so I decided to open it to at least see if I recognized where I was. There were no windows in the room except the small one in the bathroom. But it was frosted so you couldn't see in or out.

I cracked the door and all I could see was a brick wall with a shopping cart sitting in front of it. I stuck my head out a little further and I saw Jay coming around the corner. I quickly closed the door and went back to sit on the bed. As I sat there waiting for him to come back I was acutely aware of the pain I felt from my face and the migraine I felt coming on. Why would he just leave the door unlocked I thought to myself. Then I heard the doorknob turn. I laid back down on the bed trying not to think about when the bedding had been washed last.

When he entered the room I looked up and waited for him to speak I knew he was unstable and I was afraid to say the wrong thing. Well now he said you woke earlier than I expected. How is your head? Does it hurt he asked? A little I replied. Well I was at the store I picked up some Tylenol and some tequila. Ughh I said. What it's your favorite he said? Is that why you kidnapped me from the hospital and brought me to this filthy place to drink with you I asked? I thought we could talk he said but I guess I was wrong. He sat down on the other side of the bed kicked his shoes off and laid back opening a different bottle of liquor and began drinking. He grabbed a bag beside of him and said there is some sandwich stuff in there I know you are hungry he said as he tossed the bag to me. Oh and how about fixing me one too? Fix your own I mumbled.

He grabbed me by the throat and said you're an ungrateful little bitch as he slapped me. I tried to break free but I couldn't. I continued to struggle to get free as I gasped for air. The last thing I heard was him saying see what you make me do. Then I fell unconscious once again.

Jay let her fall to the bed then checked her breathing then started pacing in the tiny room that only let him take two steps then turn and start again. He was talking to himself each time he would finish a sentence he would stop and take a drink. He was no longer shaking from the alcohol withdrawal now he was scared. Scared that he would kill her if she rejected him and scared of being alone again.

He had been lying for a while he was discharged from the military when they caught him drinking on his post and they did a psychological evaluation. They told him that if he left of his own accord and continued counseling for twenty-four months they would give him an honorable discharge.

That was what had led to him beating her almost to death last time. She wasn't happy that they were about to lose everything due to his inability to cope without drinking. But he would not lose her. He deserved her respect for everything he had been through the things he had to do and see. He had fought in two wars during his military career to make it back home to her. He did love her but if he couldn't have her no one else would either. He would not be alone. She promised him forever and he to her. He had meant it when he said it and he was going to remind her of that. He never meant to hurt her and didn't understand how or why he did it himself. He was just so angry that she acted like she didn't love him anymore.

The therapist said he was bipolar and schizophrenic. That combined with his PTSD had sent him into a downward spiral. Once they had gotten him on his medication and stabilized it. He had gotten better but he didn't like the way it made him feel so he had stopped taking it and started drinking again. He would tell everyone it wasn't a big deal. He could keep the Demons at bay in the beginning but as he sat on the edge of the bed brushing her hair away from her face. Looking at the damage he had caused he felt terrible. But he also knew everything had went way to far now and there was no turning back. He was now just as much being held captive as she was he thought to himself.

CHAPTER TWENTY-FOUR

The Search

DAMN IT JONES haven't you found anything out yet? They are checking the room for prints Christian. Is that what you are waiting on we know who took her Christian said. Jones we need to be out looking for her. Where should we look Christian since you are now in charge and know more than I do Jones snapped? Anywhere, everywhere we need to do something Christian said. Jones stood there closing his eyes with two fingers squeezing the bridge of his nose.

Look Christian, I have every available officer out looking for his truck as we speak. And the private investigator is checking everywhere that he seen him go in the past month. I, we are doing everything possible right now. What I need you to do is to go home and stay by the phone if she gets loose she may try to contact you. If I find anything at all I will call you but you are just in the way here. For the first time in hours Rhonda spoke up saying Jones is right.

Fine but if you find out where he has taken her I want to be there when you get her and lock him up. Okay! Now go home Christian Jones said before walking away. Before Christian could walked away Jenifer whispered I'm sorry. Christian just put his hand up to let her know he didn't want to talk about it and continued to leave. Once Christian got home he called another friend who worked on the police force since he didn't go in for two more hours he was hoping he could catch Manuel at home. The phone rang four times before he picked up what's up bro Manuel asked? Christian quickly explained what was going on and asked Manuel if he could keep an eye out for the truck tonight on his patrol. Of course Manuel said and then said I got to go and hung up.

Meanwhile Jones had confirmed that Jays prints were all over the paper wrapped around the bouquet of flowers found on the floor. He had already known who had taken Elizabeth but he needed proof. Jays father was a rather high up Officer of the Court and he had managed time and again to keep Jay out of the system for unspeakable things. Jones knew he had to handle this carefully he understood Christian feeling like they were not moving fast enough. But Jones really wanted to get this guy and he couldn't risk him walking over some technicality.

Rhonda was now on lunch and Jenifer had went home. Rhonda sat there debating should she call her brother she wished she wasn't working today. Dr. Michaelson seen Rhonda sitting at the table in the cafeteria she was beautiful and smart and if it were not for the fear of rejection he would have asked her out seven years ago he thought to himself. But he could see the worry on her face and he wanted to be the one to take that away but he of all people knew how close her and Elizabeth had become. Elizabeth had not just another patient and they all had become close.

Dr. Michaelson, Rhonda said when she saw him still standing by the cafeteria entrance deep in thought. He looked up and said yes, hello Rhonda. How are you today he asked? Seriously he thought to himself I'm an idiot of course she not doing well he thought. I'm fine considering she said smiling. Is there anything I can do he said his face showing his concern? No she replied. I have to go and see Christian after my shift she said. Would you like some company he asked? No I'm sure you have better things to do she said. Well actually I don't and I would like to be there when you guys find out something. He was even taken back by his bluntness. Okay she said I can meet you in the parking deck at seven fifteen. Okay he said see you then he said with a big smile.

Jones was sitting at his desk trying to remember anything that Jay or Elizabeth may have told him that could help him find them. Suddenly it hit him Elizabeth talked about Jays alcohol abuse and how dependent he had become. So Jones began to search all locations with liquor stores close by. If he is as dependent on alcohol as she says he is he will be holding her somewhere alcohol is easily available, it could also be near a convenient store he thought to himself. He printed off a list of possibilities nearby and grabbed his jacket it was still coming down outside and he wouldn't be doing any good for anyone if he got sick he thought as he grabbed his keys.

At that very moment Christian was also thinking Jay would be staying close to the alcohol. He called Jones but there was no answer so he left a message and got into his Jeep to begin his own search. Him being a fireman he knew the city well. If they were in the city he would find them he thought....

CHAPTER TWENTY-FIVE

Cruel Intentions

I AWOKE SUDDENLY having ice cold water poured on my face. I opened my eyes and saw him standing over me smirking. You can't sleep all day Lizzy. My head hurt and I could feel the tightness of the swelling of my face. I sat up but said nothing. He handed me a sandwich and said you need to eat sweetie then he gave me a soda and sat down beside me.

I felt like I was going to throw up the closer he came the more I had this sickening feeling. He began speaking in a way softer tone than earlier. I am so sorry he wouldn't look at my face as he was talking to me. You just make me so mad. No one gets to me like you. I didn't do anything except tell you to make your own sandwich I said in a whisper I was trying to be careful not to anger him. That's exactly what talking about I deserve respect he said raising his voice. Do you know who I am he yelled.

I decided it was best to say nothing at all but he started to scream you don't realize who I am how could you be this stupid over and over again. I sat there saying nothing but each time he screamed I felt smaller I just wanted to cower in the corner all of my anger was gone I was scared. Christian and Jones will find me I just have to play his game until then be nice and hope he doesn't ask or expect me to do anything I really didn't want to do I thought to myself as he continued now screaming only an inch away from my face.

I said I know I am sorry please stop. Why do you do this to me he said. I don't mean to I replied. He began crying and laid his head in my lap. Just hold me he said and rub my back. That was it rub my back! Oh my god all of these memories came rushing back. I remembered.... Although a big part of me wished I didn't. That's why he almost killed me because I wouldn't rub his back! What the hell was wrong with him I thought. Lizzy are you not going to rub my back that's the least you can do he said. So I began rubbing his back lightly like I knew he liked my fingers started to tremble. I was afraid of what he might do before but now that I my memory was back I knew that he was going to kill me. But first he was going to make me pay for surviving the first time.

I now knew he was smart and that no one would find me. I sat there rubbing his back suddenly his head popped up he said just stop if you are only going to half ass rub my back just don't do it. What are you talking about? He looked at me with his hollow eyes and said it's not the same if you don't want to do it. I said I would do it I said. He said forget it I don't want you touching me your nasty he said. I am going to the store and don't try to leave because I know people around here and if I have to waste my time finding you. Let's just say you'll regret it.

I waited until he walked out the door and let out a deep breath remembering the night that put me into the hospital. I closed my eyes I could hear him screaming we had been over at the neighbor's house most of the night. We had cooked out and everyone was drinking and having a good time. We had walked home we only lived a few minutes away. When we got home I had got in the shower and he came and got in also. At first we were playing around but then it turned rough. I broke free from him and got out of the shower wrapping myself in a towel I went to the bedroom hoping he would stay in the shower.

Instead he came into the bedroom saying we are going to have sex. No we are not I replied. Then he walked over and stood in front of me every time I moved he moved staying right in my face. Will you please move out of the way I said becoming more and more agitated with him. Sure he said raising his voice I am going next door he said trying to get a reaction out of me. Next door lived a blonde she had a different guy over every other day when she seen Jay she would flirt but every time she saw me she would roll her eyes. He knew there was no love lost there so every time we argued he would bring her up. And I really didn't care anymore I just wanted him to leave. So I simply said okay.

So he left it was about eleven pm and so after putting on some night clothes I went to bed. It was two am when I woke up thirsty I figured he was asleep on the couch so I tried to be quiet but once my eyes adjusted I realized he wasn't on the couch he wasn't even home. I was a little worried about him since he was drinking but if he wanted to be stupid and get caught drinking and driving it wasn't my problem. So I went back to bed.

I didn't know what time it was when he came in but he woke me I could smell the liquor when he tried to kiss my lips I told him to go to sleep that we both needed to get some sleep. He got up and stormed off to the bathroom and slammed the door. I was having a hard time getting back to sleep but I remembered laying there pretending to be asleep hoping that would keep him off of me.

Suddenly I felt pain then I fell off of the bed or that's what I thought until I realized I was being dragged out of the bed by my hair. As soon as my brain caught up with what was happening I screamed stop please stop. I had hesitated before yelling I'm pregnant. Your what he screamed lifting me up against the wall. He began yelling louder and louder how could you do this he said. Before I could say anything he had balled his fist and began to strike. Hitting me over and over again causing me to fall to the floor with each unforgiving blow.

The last thing that I remembered was praying for him to stop. And waking up in the hospital. He knew I was pregnant... I couldn't breathe I knew I had to get out of here but now that my memory was back I knew how he worked and he was probably standing outside of the door now hoping I will try to leave. All I can do is buy time and pray that someone finds me before it's too late...

Printed in the United States
By Bookmasters